D1163845

The Nighttime Comes

CHRIS FEDORKA TOMALIN

To order additional copies of this book, contact:
Xlibris
844-714-8691
www.Xlibris.com
Orders@Xlibris.com

ISBN: Softcover 978-1-6641-5404-9
Hardcover 978-1-6641-5405-6
EBook 978-1-6641-5403-2

Print information available on the last page

Rev. date: 01/22/2021

The Nighttime Comes

CHRIS FEDORKA TOMALIN

The nighttime comes by interrupting my play,
Painting the twilight and ending my day.
Could it possibly be that those beautiful hues
can spill into dark bringing sleepy time blues?

Ten more minutes, I plead, A snack before bed?

“PJ’s on, mom repeats, Get into your bed!

Goodnight, sleep tight.”

Please keep on the light.

“It’s time that you rest. “

Black blankets the night.

They creep into my room; they slide under the door.
The monsters of darkness do their dance on my floor.
I can't look! I can't look! Pillow over my head.
I hear them! I hear them! Are they under my bed?
Why is nighttime so long? Please, God, keep my bed dry.
Is morning here yet? I ask with a sigh.

I need a drink, mom. I yell 'neath the top sheet.

"I won't say it again. It's bedtime, my sweet.

Now close those big eyes and dream some sweet dreams

of a beautiful sky, puffy clouds made of cream."

Clouds made of cream? The shadows reappear.
Some slimy green thing with a spear in his head-
I can't look! I can't look! Oh, the fear - oh the dread!

"It's your imagination," mom returns with a sigh.
Imagination? I repeat. I felt it go by.
The sweat streams down; it covers my face.
I take a quick peek - things seem in their place.

I'll keep my feet covered or they might bite off a toe.
Stay under the blanket and they're likely to go.

“Sweetie, time to wake up!” I hear my mom yell.
Is it morning already? Is that coffee I smell?
Oh, the warmth of the sun, it’s a beautiful day.
The monsters of darkness have melted away.

But where do they hide? I searched under the bed.

I went through the closet. Can it be as mom said?

Now where did they go when I woke with the light?

I sure can't explain it. Do you think that you might?

CPSIA information can be obtained
at www.ICGtesting.com
Printed in the USA
BVHW021503090321
602111BV00003B/4